Max's
Guide to Trouble!

TRULL
SHOP

C2 000 004 749221

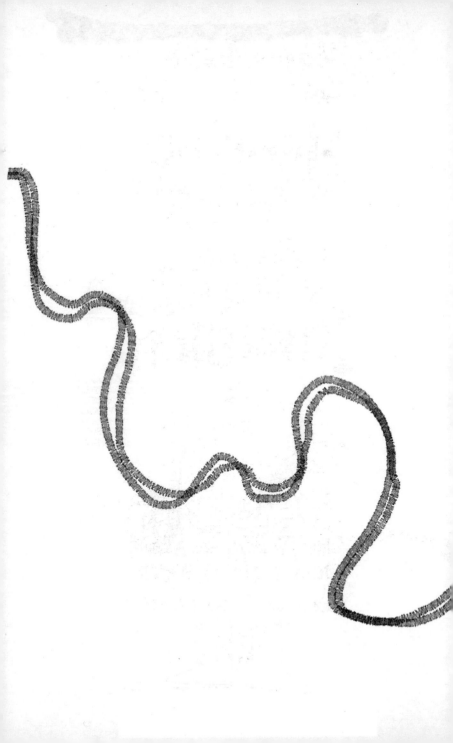

Max and Molly's Guide To Trouble:
How To stop A Viking Invasion

DOMINIC BARKER

ILLUSTRATED BY HANNAH SHAW

ORCHARD

To Emeliem Mohrer
D.B.

ORCHARD BOOKS
338 Euston Road, London NW1 3BH
Orchard Books Australia
Hachette Children's Books
Level 17/207 Kent Street, Sydney, NSW 2000

First published in 2012 by Orchard Books
ISBN 978 1 40830 522 5

Text © Dominic Barker 2012
Illustrations © Hannah Shaw 2012

The rights of Dominic Barker to be identified as the author and
Hannah Shaw to be identified as the illustrator of this work have been asserted
by them in accordance with the Copyright, Designs and Patents Act, 1988.

A CIP catalogue record for this book is available from the British Library.

1 3 5 7 9 10 8 6 4 2

Printed in the UK

Orchard Books is a division of Hachette Children's Books,
an Hachette UK company.

www.hachette.co.uk

UNSYNCHRONICITY

"Goodnight, Max. Goodnight, Molly."

"Goodnight, Mum."

"No more reading now."

"No, Mum."

Max and Molly's mum switched off the

lights in each of the two children's rooms

and went downstairs. Max and Molly began
to count. When Molly got to five hundred
she slipped out of bed, put her pink
dressing gown on over her pink pyjamas
and padded silently onto the landing.

Her twin brother, Max, was waiting.

"Where've you been?" he hissed.

"I came as soon as I got to five hundred," whispered Molly indignantly.

"You must've counted too s l o w."

"You must've counted too fast."

"Next time we'll have synchronized watches," said Max.

"Is that like synchronized swimming?" asked Molly. "Because my watch isn't waterproof."

Max sighed.

"Are you ready?"

"Isn't this **naughty**?" asked Molly.
Max shook his head.

"This is the opposite of **naughty**,"
he said. "This is good. We have to be
ready, Molly. If Trull is ever attacked by
Vikings we will be ready to spy on
them."

"But Mum said…"

"Mum said we weren't to do any more
reading. Are you doing any reading?"

Molly shook her head.

"Neither am I," said Max. "Now hurry
up! We've been studying the Vikings

at school in history. They could return at
any moment to pillage Trull."

Molly disagreed.

"If **Vikings** are in history we don't need to worry about them."

Max shook his head.

"That's just what people want you to think," he told his sister. "But what about the NORMANS? They invaded Trull in 1066. It's on the Bayeux Tapestry. That was in history."

"So?" said Molly.

"There are two NORMANS in our class," said Max. "NORMAN Kay and NORMAN Marshall. So just because things are in history doesn't mean they can't be in our time too."

Molly couldn't argue with this. The NORMANS really were here. She wondered what an army of NORMANS would look like. Would they be different from an army of **Henrys**?

"Molly!" said Max. "Hurry up! They could be getting into their longboats in a fjord somewhere."

"Who?"

Max shook his head. Molly could never remember anything important.

"The **Vikings!**"

IF ONLY...

Max and Molly's parents were sitting
on the sofa watching the TV.

"I can't stand these reality shows,"
said Dad. "Why can't we watch the
documentary on the other side?"

"I'm watching this," insisted Mum.

"The documentary's about **crop rotation in allotments**," Dad persisted.

Behind them, the sitting-room door opened slightly. Silently, Max and Molly crawled in.

"**Allotments**?" said Mum. I am *not* watching anything about **allotments**."

"Is there a draught in here?" said Dad.

Behind the sofa, Max and Molly froze.

"That door has never fitted properly," said Mum. "You said you'd mend it before the twins were born."

"It's on my list."

"They're eight."

"It's a long list."

Max took out two tiny pieces of paper from his pyjama pocket and handed one to Molly. Then he held up three fingers and counted down:

Three...two...one...go!

Max and Molly rose up behind their parents. Carefully, they each placed a small

piece of paper on their parents' heads.
Mission accomplished. They disappeared.

"I'm worried about Max and Molly," said
Mum as the reality show went to a break
for adverts. "If only they could be more
like the Goodleys' children. They're so
POLITE and WELL-BEHAVED."

Dad scoffed. "Benedict and Imogen Goodley!" he said. "Let's not get too carried away. Our children are never going to be *anything like* the Goodleys."

Behind the sofa, Max and Molly nodded to each other – they agreed there was no chance of them ever being anything like the Goodleys.

They were about to crawl into the hall when they heard one more thing.

"I suppose," admitted Mum ruefully. "But to have children like the Goodleys – even just for one day. Wouldn't that be wonderful?"

The sitting-room door closed. Max and Molly snuck back upstairs.

"That draught again!" said Mum. "If you don't get it fixed tomorrow then I'm getting a man in to do it."

"I'm a man," protested Dad.

"I meant a proper man."

"I'm a proper man."

"Of course you're not," said Mum, turning to look at him. "A proper man doesn't have bits of paper on his head."

Dad couldn't think of an answer.

CAREFUL WHAT YOU WISH FOR

"I don't understand," said Molly the next morning after breakfast. "If the **Vikings** invade Trull, I don't see what use it will be to sneak up and put bits of paper on their heads."

"It's *training*," Max explained. "When

the **Vikings** really invade we'll have to sneak up on them and fight them. But I didn't want to fight Mum and Dad."

"No," agreed Molly. "Then they would have known we'd got out of bed and we wouldn't have got any pocket money this week."

"We're not getting any pocket money this week anyway," Max reminded her. "Because of the thing with Peter's moustache."

"Plus the ABOMINABLE SNOWMAN," remembered Molly sadly. "If only we could do something good they might change their mind about the pocket money."

They both fell into deep thought.

"I know," said Max suddenly. "Do you remember what Mum said last night?"

"She said she wished we were more like the Goodleys."

21

"Exactly."

"She didn't mean it, did she?" said Molly in horror.

"She sounded like she did. If we're going to get any pocket money, then we're going to have to try it."

"But I don't know how to be like the Goodleys," protested Molly.

"Not yet," Max said. "So we're going to make them teach us."

ANOTHER WORLD

The doorbell rang at the Goodleys' house.

"Can I go and answer it, Daddy?" said
Benedict Goodley.

"Oh, please let me, Daddy," said Imogen
Goodley.

"I've a better idea," said their father

with an indulgent smile.

"We could both answer it!" chorused Benedict and Imogen.

"Run along then," said their father. "But don't run too fast. That would be dangerous."

Benedict and Imogen ran very **SAFELY** towards the front door. They opened it with big welcoming smiles on their faces.

"Hello," said Max and Molly.

"Er...hello," answered Benedict and Imogen, their welcoming smiles turning into nervous grins. They had played with Max and Molly once before and it was the only time in their entire lives they had got in **trouble**.

"We need you to do us a favour," Max told them.

Benedict and Imogen looked at each other even more nervously. But they had always been told by their parents to help people who asked for it. So they resolved to make the best of it.

"Always happy to do a favour for a friend, aren't we, Imogen?" said Benedict as heartily as he could manage.

"Too right, Benedict," agreed Imogen, a little too quickly. "What is it?"

"We want to be you," explained Molly briefly.

SPELLING IT OUT

Max and Molly were shown into
Benedict and Imogen's bedroom. It was
spotless. Books were arranged
alphabetically on the shelves, every toy
was stacked evenly and every item of
clothing was neatly hung up.

"Is it always like this?" said Molly.

Imogen nodded.

Molly took out the notebook that she'd brought with her especially so they could remember all the things they needed to do. She wrote:

Being Benedict and Imogen
Rule 1:
Kkkeep bedroom tidy
at all times

"Is there a spelling mistake there?" asked Benedict.

Molly shook her head. She had her own personal form of spelling. It had developed after she had heard in assembly that you should always make a special effort to include people in your games who didn't get to play much. Molly thought this was such good advice that she had decided to extend it to other parts of her life too. Including spelling. She had decided that letters like K and Z and q, which weren't used as often as other letters, ought to be more involved, so on the rare occasions they appeared she used them more than once so they didn't feel unpopular.

"What else do you do?" Max asked.

"Well," said Benedict. "I was just thinking that it's time for my oboe practice."

"And my violin practice," added Imogen.

"Sometimes we play together," said Benedict. "Would you like to hear us?"

"Couldn't we just imagine?" said Molly.

It turned out they couldn't. Benedict and Imogen played a very pretty duet that lasted for five minutes, but to Max and Molly it felt quite a lot longer. During the performance Molly wrote in her notebook:

Rule 2:
Play a muzzikkal instrument

Sometimes, Molly substituted popular letters with the lonely ones.

"Very nice," said Max when Benedict and Imogen stopped. Now you've got to teach us how to play it so we can be you."

Benedict and Imogen looked doubtful.

"It's not that easy," said Benedict.

"Pass it over," said Max, confidently reaching for the oboe.

Molly took Imogen's violin. Together Max and Molly began to play. They produced a sound of screeching strings plus a mixture of blowing and wheezing.

Even Max and Molly, who were normally able to interpret almost anything they did as a success, were forced to admit that their first performance was **less** than a TRIUMPH.

"Are there any other things we could play?" asked Molly.

"Where you don't have to blow," gasped Max, whose face had turned an alarming shade of red.

"And that you could learn in less than a day."

Benedict and Imogen racked their brains. They quickly rejected the GUITAR, the piano,

the **drums**. Finally they came
up with...

"The spoons!"

"spoons?" repeated Molly doubtfully.

"I thought you ate **jelly** with spoons."

Imogen explained that you could also bang
two spoons together against your knee as
a musical instrument.

"I think I'd prefer **jelly**," said Molly.

But Max immediately saw the potential for the two of them to make a swift advance in their quest to become more like the Goodleys. He and Benedict rushed off to the kitchen to get some SpOOnS.

"While the boys are gone," said Imogen conspiratorially, "why don't we practise our times tables?"

BITTERSWEET SYMPHONY

"What is that racket?" cried Benedict's father.

He threw down his paper, stomped upstairs and flung open the door to Benedict and Imogen's room.

And found himself witnessing the

world premiere of the Laburnam Avenue Symphony in D Minor for oboe, violin and spoons.

As soon as he appeared, Benedict and Imogen noticed his cross face and stopped playing. There followed a short spoon solo from Max and Molly. Then they stopped too.

"I am sorry, Daddy," said Benedict.

"I'm sorry too," said Imogen.

"You have very clean SpOOnS," said Molly.

Mr Goodley regretted his brief loss of temper.

"Don't apologise, children, don't apologise," he said. "It's good to see you experimenting with new musical forms. Young people like yourselves are the future of the creative arts. Did Mozart think of using SpOOnS? Did Beethoven?"

"Probably for **jelly**," said Molly.

"Perhaps," agreed Mr Goodley. "But you have realised that **spoons** are so much more than cutlery. You have unlocked their inner voice. I shall leave you to discover more, *mes enfants*."

Mr Goodley went downstairs thinking how wonderful children were. He was so cheerful that he decided to treat himself to a walk around his immaculately tended garden.

Meanwhile, upstairs, liberated by parental approval, Max and Molly were playing the SPOONS with ever more enthusiasm. They banged them on their arms, on their heads, on the walls, against the desk – anything to get a different sound.

It was when doing a particularly
vigorous beating on the radiator
that the SPOONS slipped
out of Max's hand and
flew up and out
of the open
bedroom window.

Down below, Mr Goodley was enjoying the sweet smell of the flowers. The roses were looking wonderful, the sweet peas were exploding with colour, the tulips were swaying in the light breeze and as for the crocuses they were—

A SPOON landed on Mr Goodleys head.

"Ow!"

He looked up. Four faces looked down at him.

"Sorry, Daddy!" said Benedict.

"Really sorry, Daddy!" added Imogen.

"If stung by a Portuguese Man o' War it is advisable to immerse the affected part in hot water," said Max.

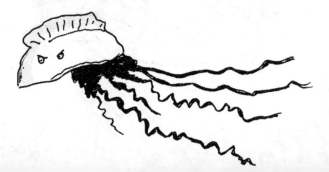

"We're going to need a cleaner spoon," said Molly.

Mr Goodly reconsidered his approach to experimental music.

"No more spoons!" he announced. "If the instrument is not in a standard orchestra then I believe it has no place in my home."

Max sighed. He'd been hoping to try and play the **cheeseboard** next.

FIND THE CAUSE!

"Apart from tidying your bedroom and music practice," Max asked after the **spoons** had been recovered, washed and placed carefully in the cutlery drawer, "what else do you do?"

"Like something outside?" suggested Molly.

Max nodded. There were always more interesting things to do outside.

"Oh yes," said Benedict. "We like to go outside and help people."

Max and Molly brightened up. Helping sounded far more interesting than tidying.

"Let's do that!" said Max.

The children ran down the stairs and out into the street. Benedict and Imogen were running safely so they got there a little after Max and Molly, who went everywhere at top speed

Apart from to bed when it was bedtime.

"Who do we help?" asked Max when Benedict and Imogen arrived. "Can we help anyone?"

Benedict shook his head.

"It is very important that whoever we help is a 𝒢ood 𝒞ause."

"Am I a 𝒢ood 𝒞ause?" wondered Molly.

"I don't think so," said Imogen. "Are you Needy?"

"I am at tea time," said Molly.

"That's just hungry," said Benedict.
"It's different."

"Needy," explained Imogen, "is people who are less fortunate than you."

"Like our friend, Peter," suggested Max.

"Why's he Needy?"

"He's always getting colds."

Benedict and Imogen considered this and decided that always getting colds wasn't quite Needy enough.

"We'll have to stick to our normal solution when looking for Needy people," said Benedict.

"What's that?"

"Find an old person."

NEEDING THE NEEDY

Old people, according to Benedict and Imogen, were always Needy and so the children set to work immediately to locate one. But it seemed that **old** people were just like buses: whenever you didn't need one they were everywhere, but as soon as you wanted one there were none to be found.

"Let's go towards the shops," suggested Benedict. "Then we can help them with their shopping on the way back."

They were about to cross over the road to continue the search when there was a **growling** sound in the distance. Moments later, around the corner roared a large motorbike ridden by a big man wearing a leather jacket and a helmet. His blond hair flowed out from underneath it and blew in the wind as he powered

down Ash Grove. However, when he saw
the children he suddenly brought his bike
to a screeching halt alongside them.

He took off his helmet. He was about
twenty-seven, with deep blue eyes and
muscles everywhere.

"Hi, Benedict. Hi, Imogen," said the motorcyclist. He had a slightly unusual accent that Max and Molly had never heard before.

"Hi, Erik," said Benedict.

"This is **Erik Eriksson**," Imogen told Max and Molly. "He runs the under-10s Canoe and Kayak club."

"Are you Needy?" Max asked him.

Erik misheard Max's question.

"Am I from Norway?" he said. "Yes I am. How did you know?"

Molly misheard Erik's answer.

Or at least she pretended to. As far as she was concerned, Erik had just confirmed he was Needy.

"Can we help you cross the road?" she asked.

"No, thank you," said Erik. He turned his attention to Benedict and Imogen. "I wanted to tell you that because of a personal matter the Canoe and Kayak club will be held on Thursday rather than Wednesday. Is that OK?"

"That will be fine," they both told Erik.

"Great!" said Erik.

While they were talking a curious expression had appeared on Max's face.

"So you like boats?" he asked Erik.

Erik nodded enthusiastically.

"My job is in computers," he told the children. "It means I am indoors all the time. So I love the opportunity to get out on the water after work. You can join the club if you like."

But Max didn't hear this kind offer.

"Do you prefer long boats or short boats?" he asked Erik.

"Oh, long boats," answered Erik. "I'm tall and they have more leg room."

"Hmm," said Max suspiciously.

"Oh no!" said Erik suddenly, looking at his watch. "I've got to get to the jewellers. See you on Thursday!"

And he roared off on his huge motorbike.

"Comes from Norway and likes long boats and jewellery," thought Max. "I wonder..."

"Look!" cried Molly. "An **old** lady!"

His sister was right. There was an **old** lady shuffling along in the distance.

Even better, she was carrying two bags.

"Hurrah!" said Benedict and Imogen.

"Stop her before she gets away,"
said Max

The **old** lady in question was
Mrs Quibble and even the most charitable
observer would have to admit that her
"getting away" days were long behind her.
Nevertheless Max and Molly pursued her at
high speed.

"Can we help you with your shopping?"

Mrs Quibble eyed Max and Molly warily.

"No, thank you," she said. "I haven't
got very much to carry."

"Could you go and buy some more things?" asked Molly.

"I beg your pardon, young..."

But Mrs Quibble was distracted by the arrival of the Goodleys, who ran up at a sensible pace.

"Good morning, Mrs Quibble," they chorused.

Mrs Quibble, like every old lady in the neighbourhood, loved Benedict and Imogen.

"Hello!" she beamed down at them.

"Have you got over your cold?" asked Benedict kindly.

"I think so," Mrs Quibble told him.

"Is that a new perm?" asked Imogen. "Blue does suit you."

"Do you think so, dear? I don't know if I'm a bit old for it."

Imogen shook her head.

"It looks wonderful," she told Mrs Quibble.

"Can we help with your shopping?" asked Benedict.

"That's very kind of you, my dear," said Mrs Quibble.

She handed one bag over to Benedict and one to Imogen.

"Hey!" protested Max. "That's not fair. You said no when we asked you. Why can they help you if we can't?"

"Benedict and Imogen did not charge up to me and demand my shopping bag without so much as howdoyoudo," said Mrs Quibble. "They were polite and friendly and put my mind at rest about a personal issue."

"You mean your blue head," said Molly.

"Hair," corrected Imogen.

Max was confused.

"But we were trying to help the Needy," he explained. "We didn't know you had to talk to the Needy too."

"How dare you say I'm Needy?" Mrs Quibble snapped. "I am nothing of the sort. Come, Benedict and Imogen."

Max and Molly looked at each other.

Helping the Needy was going to be harder than they thought.

HOW TO TALK TO GROWN-UPS

"You can't just start helping people straight away," said Benedict. "You've got to win their trust first."

The Goodleys had returned from Mrs Quibble's house, each with a shiny pound coin as a reward for their efforts.

Molly took out her notebook and
wrote down:

Rule 3:
Help the Needy only
after they trust you zqzk.

If there wasn't a word in a sentence with
an unusual letter then Molly often added a
made up one at the end.

"How do you make them trust you?"
asked Max.

"You have to talk to them," explained Benedict.

"Talk to them?" said Max. "What about?"

"The weather," said Imogen. "Grown-ups love talking about the weather."

"Or their health," said Benedict. "Those are the two things that grown-ups like talking about more than anything else."

"And the colour of their head," Molly remembered.

"I'd stick to the weather and health," said Benedict.

"We could just go and spend your

pounds on SWEETS and FIZZY DRINKS instead," suggested Molly.

Benedict and Imogen recoiled in horror.

"SWEETS!" they said together.

"What about your teeth?"

"What about them?" said Molly.

"They'll rot and fall out," said Benedict. "We can't spend it on SWeets. Whenever we get money we give it to Daddy."

"Why?" said Max.

"For our pension," said Benedict.

"Your what?" said Molly.

"Our pension," repeated Benedict. "Daddy says it's never too soon to start making provisions for your **old** age."

"Our pocket money goes straight into it too," said Imogen proudly.

Molly opened her notebook extremely reluctantly.

Rule 4:
Put pocket money in
a pension xkzq.

"I don't care how much Mum wants it," Max confided to Molly in a whisper. "I don't think we can be like the Goodleys."

"But she only wants us to be like them for a day," whispered back Molly. "We'll just make sure that it's not a Saturday."

Saturday was the day they got their pocket money.

Just as Max was realising the cleverness of Molly's plan, **old** Mr Everett came round the corner of Copper Beech Lane with his dog, Snowy. He was carrying two shopping bags.

This was Max and Molly's chance!

"Remember," cautioned Benedict. "Get him to trust you first! The weather and health."

Max and Molly set off repeating "Weather, health, weather, health" to themselves again and again and again.

This time there would be no mistakes.

KETCH UP!

Old Mr Everett saw Max and Molly coming. He crossed the road. The last time they'd spoken to him his dog had ended up ten different colours and his garden had been destroyed.

But Max and Molly were not to be so

easily deterred. They crossed the road too.

"Hello, Mr Everett," said Max.

"Hello, Snowy," said Molly.

Mr Everett nodded warily

at Max and Snowy

licked Molly's hand.

"Can we have..." began Max. And then he stopped himself. Weather and health first, he remembered.

"I must be getting back," said Mr Everett. "I don't want my peas to defrost."

"Wait a minute," said Max. "We have to talk about the weather."

"Ah! The weather," said Mr Everett, seeming to relax a bit. "I think there might be a spot of drizzle later."

Max felt that if you had to talk about the weather you should at least inject a little more excitement into it.

"There are no **hurricanes** forecast,"
he informed Mr Everett. "But if there
were you could expect winds of over one
hundred miles an hour and driving rain.
Your house might well suffer significant
damage."

Mr Everett looked a little apprehensive. **Hurricanes**? In Trull?

"But," added Max, "a **tornado** might be even worse. Your house could lose its roof."

"And then your stuff might get wet when it drizzled later," added Molly.

Mr Everett's brow furrowed with worry. Max sensed that weather was not winning his trust. He decided to try health instead.

"Is your **typhoid** clearing up?"

"**Typhoid**?" said a startled Mr Everett. "I don't have **typhoid**."

"How about your cholera?"

"Cholera?" said Mr Everett. "Who's got cholera?"

Max was disappointed. Mr Everett did not appear to be recovering from any major diseases. He decided to try something simpler.

"Have you got any **warts**?" he asked.

"Or bunions?" suggested Molly.

Mr Everett had had enough of these insolent questions.

"I must get my fish fingers in the freezer," he told them.

Unfortunately, Max and Molly heard this as an appeal from a Needy person who was worried about his shopping being ruined. Convinced they had won old Mr Everett's trust, they leapt forward eagerly to assist.

"We'll carry them for you!"

"We'll get them back for you really fast!"

Believing that Mr Everett had already
asked for help they each grabbed one bag.
But Mr Everett didn't think he'd asked
for help.

"What do you think you're doing?"
he cried. "Thieves!"

It was at this moment that, on
his regular daily beat, PC Truncheon
turned into Copper Beech Lane and
saw two children, each pulling a bag of
shopping from a defenceless old person.
PC Truncheon started to run.

Meanwhile, Max and Molly realised

their mistake and immediately let go of
Mr Everett's shopping bags. Unfortunately
he was tugging them back with such force
that their contents flew out and landed
in the road.

"We'll pick them up for you," said Max.

"Leave my shopping alone," he protested. "I'm a pensioner."

By now PC Truncheon was thundering down the lane.

"Mugging in process!" he shouted into his radio. PC Truncheon sped past the Goodleys, who were watching with open-mouthed astonishment at what was going on. It didn't seem as though things could get any more chaotic.

But then Molly grabbed a bottle of
tomato ketchup from the ground. It was
a squeezy bottle and the top had been
knocked off. As she picked it up, she
squeezed it by accident. A great big gob
of tomato ketchup splurged onto Snowy.

From halfway down the lane, PC
Truncheon saw a red blob appear out
of nowhere on the white dog. To PC
Truncheon, who had only this morning
been reading a leaflet about terrorist
threats, it could only be one thing...

Blood.

"Dog wounded!" he yelled into his
radio. "I repeat, dog down. This is now a
shooting incident. Back-up required!"

THERMIDORIAN REACTION

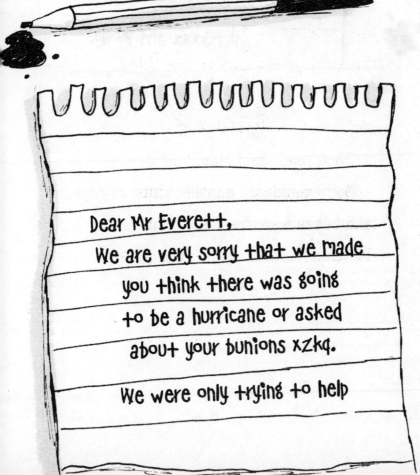

Dear Mr Everett,
We are very sorry that we made
you think there was going
to be a hurricane or asked
about your bunions xzkq.

We were only trying to help

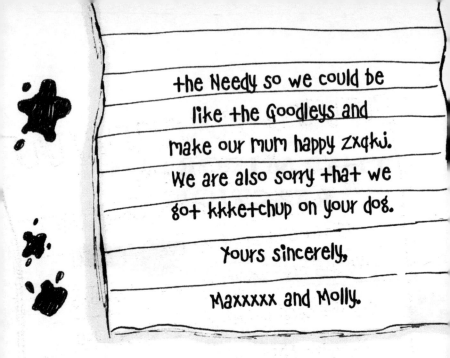

the Needy so we could be
like the Goodleys and
make our mum happy zxqkj.
We are also sorry that we
got kkketchup on your dog.

Yours sincerely,

Maxxxxxx and Molly.

"Next one," said Max.

Molly picked up another sheet of paper
and began to write.

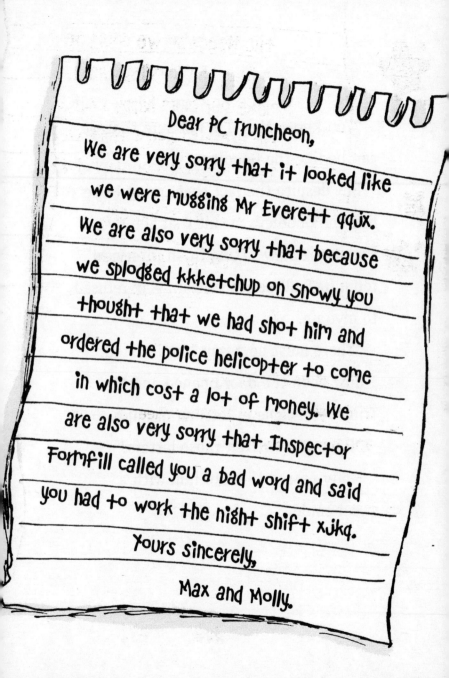

Dear PC Truncheon,

We are very sorry that it looked like we were mugging Mr Everett qqux. We are also very sorry that because we splodged kkketchup on Snowy you thought that we had shot him and ordered the police helicopter to come in which cost a lot of money. We are also very sorry that Inspector Formfill called you a bad word and said you had to work the night shift xjkq.

Yours sincerely,

Max and Molly.

"You know, Max. I'm not sure that we can be like the Goodleys."

But despite the fact that trying to be like the Goodleys meant that the two of them were now sitting in an interview room in Trull police station, Max refused to give up.

"There must be a way," he insisted.

Just then the door opened and PC Truncheon came in looking grumpy.

"Have you written those letters?"

Molly passed them to him with a sweet smile.

The sweet smile had no effect on PC Truncheon. He glanced at their letters.

"You're both very lucky Benedict and Imogen Goodley backed up your story," he said. "Now get along with you."

He led the children out of the interview room. In the corridor they almost banged into a blond man dressed in leathers and carrying a motorbike helmet.

Erik Eriksson. He stopped to talk to PC Truncheon.

"You shouldn't have any more problems with the computers," he said. "I've done a full virus scan."

"Thank you," said PC Truncheon. "At least one part of my day has gone smoothly."

"I tell you something," **Erik Eriksson** said. "I need the rest of my day to go smoothly. Something very important is going to happen."

"What is it?" asked PC Truncheon.

"It's a secret," said Erik with a wink. "A very big secret."

Max pricked up his ears.

"Do you ever get homesick for Norway?" asked PC Truncheon.

"Sometimes," admitted Erik. "I miss the dark and the herring and the ridiculously high standard of living."

"What about your family and friends?"

"I miss them too," said Erik. "But if my secret goes well then I'll be seeing all my family and my friends soon. And not in Norway. They'll all be coming to Trull!"

Max's ears pricked up even further.

"But now I must be going," said **Erik Eriksson**. "There is a lot of preparation to do if this secret thing is to be a success."

And he rushed off.

PC Truncheon led the children to the door of the police station.

"Don't let me hear of you getting into any more mischief," he said sternly.

"We won't," Molly assured him. "Will we, Max?"

Max, his mind still on other things, followed Molly. She led the way home as it was almost lunch time. When they got back to Laburnum Avenue they found their mum standing in the road and talking to Mrs Goodley.

"Benedict and Imogen have so many demands on their time," Mrs Goodley was telling Mum. "If it's not the woodcraft folk, it's the music. If it's not the origami, it's the sailing."

"Mmmm," said Mum.

"And if it's none of them, it's the **Mandarin Chinese**."

"**Mandarin Chinese**?" Mum couldn't stop herself asking.

"Their father believes that with the global economy developing in the way it is, a thorough grounding in the **Mandarin** language will give Benedict and Imogen a real advantage in the future."

"Hmmm," said Mum.

"I suppose it's the same with Max and Molly," said Mrs Goodley.

"Not quite the same," admitted Mum.

"Still, must be getting along now," said Mrs Goodley. "My lobster thermidor won't make itself."

Mrs Goodley went indoors. Mum shook her head and said something to herself – it sounded a bit like "Hope you choke on your lobster".

Then she noticed Max and Molly.

"Where have you been this morning?"

"We've been running away from the police helicopter," said Molly sweetly.

"What have I told you about not telling the truth, young lady?" said their mum.

PILLAGING PENSIONS!

"I've got it!" said Max.

It was after lunch and Max and Molly were in the garden.

"I know how we can be more like the Goodleys."

"I'm not putting all my pocket money

in a pension," Molly protested.

"No, Molly," Max said. "We won't be like the Goodleys like they are now."

Molly didn't understand. "But Mum said she wanted us to be like them."

"Yes," Max nodded. "And one way we could be like them would be if we acted more like them. But the other way would be if they acted more like us. Then we could be like them without even changing."

Molly's mouth fell open in admiration. It was brilliant.

"And I know how we can help them
be like us and save Trull from the
Vikings at the same time," said Max.
"Come on!"

They rushed across the road and rang
the Goodleys' bell.

Benedict and Imogen answered it
together. They seemed to both take a
step back when they saw it was Max
and Molly.

"Oh," said Benedict. "Hello."

"Hello," said Max. "Do you want
to come out?"

"Only if you promise not to go near anybody Needy," said Benedict.

"Or upset any policeman," said Imogen.

"That was just an accident," Molly assured them. "We're all friends again now."

"And no more helicopters," they both said.

Max and Molly agreed to these terms.

"What would you like to play?" Benedict asked. "**Musical appreciation**?"

Max shook his head.

"We haven't got time to play. We've got to stop the Viking invasion."

"The **Viking** Invasion?" said Benedict, looking puzzled. "But the **Vikings** haven't invaded for over a thousand years."

"They've been lulling us into a false sense of security," explained Max. "Now, when we least expect it, they'll launch their longboats and come **pillaGinG**."

"What's **pillaGinG**?" asked Imogen.

"**PillaGinG** means to strip ruthlessly of money or goods by open violence," said Benedict, whose hobbies included reading the dictionary.

"Wouldn't it be best to report it to the police?" asked Imogen.

"Not yet," said Max, shaking his head. "First we need more evidence, and second we need to wait until PC Truncheon's started on the nightshift. He probably isn't going to listen to us at the moment because of the whole helicopter thing."

"But where will we find evidence?" Imogen wanted to know.

"Aha!" said Max. "I've already spotted a **Viking** scout in Trull."

"Who?" The other three were goggle-eyed with excitement. A real **Viking** in Trull!

"**Erik Eriksson**," said Max.

The other three's eyes ungoggled.

"But he coaches the Canoe and Kayak club," said Benedict.

"That's just to keep in practice," insisted Max.

"Practice for what?"

"For the rest of the time – when he's a **Viking**."

Benedict and Imogen were not convinced.

"We thought he was a computer programmer."

"You don't expect him to just tell you he's a **Viking**, do you?" Max said scornfully. "He's got to pretend to be something else until his raiding party arrives."

But to Max's amazement Benedict and Imogen were still not convinced. They demanded more evidence.

"He's from Norway," Max pointed out. "He likes long boats. And jewellery. And he wears a helmet."

"That's because he's got a motorbike," said Benedict.

"That's what he wants you to think," Max insisted. "I bet his helmet has detachable horns."

"I'm not sure..." began Benedict.

But Max was by now in full flow.

"You weren't at the police station," he told them. "Me and Molly heard him say that he's got a big secret and if all goes well all his family and friends will come to Trull. I worked it out. They are all **Vikings** and they are about to attack."

Benedict and Imogen still seemed unsure that a **Viking** invasion was imminent.

"I can prove it to you," Max told them. "But don't blame me if the whole of Trull has been **pillaGed** in the meantime and we all have to pay our pocket money as **Danegeld.**"

"**Danegeld?**" said Benedict, who when he wasn't reading the dictionary, could often be found learning obscure facts from his encyclopaedia. "You mean the tax exacted by the **Vikings** in return for no longer sending raiding parties?"

"Exactly," said Max. "What will become of your pension then?"

The threat to their pension was enough for Benedict and Imogen. They agreed to accompany Max and Molly to defeat the Viking invasion.

ERIK'S HEDGE

Erik Eriksson had lived in a small house on Larch Street for the last two years, since riding his huge motorbike over from Norway to settle in Trull. His motorbike was always clean, but today it was even more polished and sparkly than usual, because today was

a very special day. Today was the day
he was going to ask his girlfriend, Emma,
to marry him.

An alley ran alongside Erik's house,
which served as a shortcut between Park
Road and Larch Street. A thick hedge
ran along its entire length. It meant that
nobody could peer into Erik's garden
from the alley, but it also meant that he
couldn't see who was there. It was into this
alley that Max, Molly, Benedict and Imogen
silently wheeled their bikes, laid them
carefully against the hedge and waited.

Erik had made sure everything was
perfect. He had trimmed his blond beard.
He had tied his long blond hair into a neat
ponytail. He had taken out the engagement
ring and looked at it time
and time again. Would she like it?
Oh, how he hoped she would! He and Emma
were compatible in every way but one.
She didn't like riding on the back of his
motorbike and all his life Erik had dreamt

of leaving his wedding and riding off into the sunset with his new bride sitting behind him.

His mobile phone rang.

Behind the hedge, Max signalled for the others to be extra silent.

"Hello," they heard Erik say.

At least that was what they thought they heard him say. Erik retained a Norwegian accent, which sometimes made words difficult to understand. Especially from behind a hedge.

"Come round now," said Erik. "I want to take you for a journey on my motorbike."

Erik sighed as he listened to Emma's reply.

"I know that you don't like the motorbike," he said, "but this time I will go so very slowly. You will see that

there is no better thing to do than be
pillaGinG!"

Max turned immediately to the others.
From their horrified faces he could see
they had all heard the word.

Erik Eriksson was talking about
pillaGinG!

"You'll be round in five minutes?" they
heard Erik say to Emma. "Great!"

On the other side of the hedge,
Max, Molly, Benedict and Imogen were
frantically trying to communicate with one
another using their hands because

they didn't want to alert Erik to their presence by talking. After five minutes of vigorous arm waving and hand signals, Max thought they were going to follow Erik, Benedict thought they were going to the police, Imogen thought they were staying in the alley, and Molly thought they were doing all three.

Before they could sort it out, there were voices from the other side of the fence.

"Hello!"

"Emma! You have brought your crash helmet?"

"Remember you promised to go really slowly."

"I remember."

"Because if you don't I'm getting off and going home."

"Don't worry," said Erik.

There was a roar as the motorbike fired

into life. And Erik, with Emma on the back, drove into Larch Street.

"Come on!" said Max.

"He's on a motorbike," said Benedict. "We can't keep up with him."

"He's a **Viking** going **pillaGinG**," said Max. "We have to try."

A ROCK AND A SOGGY PLACE

If the children had been following Erik on a normal day, they wouldn't have seen him for dust as his powerful bike roared off into the distance. But for Erik this was anything but a normal day. Knowing Emma's nervousness, he drove his bike at

the slowest speed he could manage.
At least it felt slow to him. But then his
bike had an engine.

Pedalling furiously behind it felt
anything but slow to Max, Molly, Benedict
and Imogen. They whizzed down Larch
Street, zoomed along Copper Beech Lane
and toiled up Trull Hill. Every time they
turned into a road, Erik's bike was turning
out of it, and they had to ride harder and
harder to keep him in sight.

The motorbike turned left and chugged

down Watery Way, the road that led to the river. Using the last of their energy, Max, Molly, Benedict and Imogen pedalled hard behind them.

Watery Way was a dead end. Erik parked his bike and he and Emma clambered off.

Max, Molly, Benedict and Imogen hung back until they'd walked off a little way, then they got off their bikes and snuck up to Erik's motorbike. It was so big that there was room for all of them to hide behind it.

They had an excellent view as Erik
led Emma down to the riverbank. But
unfortunately they were too far away for
the children to hear anything and if they
tried to get nearer then they would be
spotted.

"This doesn't look much like pillaGinG," whispered Benedict.

"It's not started yet," said Max. "He's probably waiting until the rest of the ViKings get here with their longboat. That's why he's brought her to the river."

"Do you think the River Piddle is big enough for a longboat?" asked Imogen.

Max nodded.

"That's what makes the **Vikings** so cunning," he explained knowledgeably. "If they'd have built fatboats they'd have got stuck."

Meanwhile Erik was building up to the biggest question of his life. He had brought Emma to this idyllic spot where ducklings dabbled and dragonflies buzzed. He had compared Emma's eyes favourably with the blue of the river.

He had compared her laugh
favourably with the sound
of the babbling water.
He got down on
one knee.

"Ow!"

He'd knelt on
a thistle.

"What's the matter?" asked Emma.

There were tears in Erik's eyes.
Partly because of the heightened
emotion of the moment, but mainly
because of the thistle. He made himself

ignore the pain, reached into his
pocket and pulled out the ring.
By now his back was to the children
so they didn't see it.

"Will you marry me, Emma?"

Emma looked deep into Erik's eyes.

"Yes!"

Overcome with joy and desperate to get
his knee off the thistle, Erik leapt to his
feet, grasped Emma's hand and thrust the
ring onto her finger. Then he puckered
his lips for a kiss. But he didn't get one.

"That's not my engagement finger," said

Emma. "It should go on the fourth finger, not the middle one."

Erik couldn't believe that he'd made such a stupid mistake. He tried to pull the ring off, but middle fingers are bigger than fourth fingers and the ring wouldn't come. Erik tugged harder.

"Ow!" cried Emma. "You're hurting me!"

Max, Molly, Benedict and Imogen heard this cry of distress.

"Straighten your finger," ordered Erik. "Then I can get your ring off."

"He's **pillaGiNG** her ring!" shouted Max. "We've got to save her. Come on."

Max, Molly, Benedict and Imogen charged towards the **Viking** and his victim. Erik and Emma were so involved in shouting at each other and tugging at the ring that they didn't see them coming. The four children ran down the riverbank and

simultaneously smashed into Erik.
He let go of Emma's hand. He toppled
backwards and...

SPLOSH!

Fell into the river.

There were a number of critical quacks
from some passing ducklings.

"What are you doing?" shouted Emma.
"Rescuing you from the **Vikings**,"
Max informed her, noticing that the ring
was still on her finger and congratulating
himself on a job well done.

With a splutter **Erik Eriksson**'s head
resurfaced in the river.

"What was that for?" he demanded.

"We heard you planning," Max told him. "On the phone. You said there's nothing better to do than be **pillaGinG**. And here you are **pillaGinG** a ring."

"**PillaGinG**?" cried Erik. "I didn't say that. I said 'be on the pillion'."

"Pillion!" cried Benedict, remembering the dictionary definition with horror. "To ride on the back of a motorbike!"

"But you were stealing her ring!" protested Max.

"I was trying to get the ring on the right finger," said Erik.

"He'd just asked me to marry him," confirmed Emma.

"But in the police station you said all your family and friends would soon be here," insisted Max. "Explain that!"

"They'll be coming to the wedding,"
said Erik.

It appeared he had explained it.

There was a short silence.

"You're sure you're not a **Viking**?"
said Max.

The ducks quacked. The dragonflies
buzzed.

"Would you like some help, out of the river?"

Max was about to try and help, but Molly stopped him. She remembered that with the Needy you had to do something first.

"Do you think it's going to rain later?" she asked Erik. "I hope not because standing in that river you'll probably catch a cold."

And now, having won the trust of the Needy, she allowed Max to go and help Erik out of the water.

A SORT OF HAPPY ENDING

"I cannot say just how sorry I am,
Mr **Eriksson** and Ms Robbins. You can
be sure I take this kind of behaviour
extremely seriously, and they will both
receive severe tellings-off and their pocket
money will be docked. May I take this

opportunity to wish you congratulations on your engagement. Mr Pesker and I will of course be sending a substantial present round tomorrow. Goodbye."

Mum watched Erik and Emma walk down the drive. Then she shut the door and marched into the living room, where Molly and Max were sitting nervously.

"Right then, you two, you have got some explaining to..."

She stopped. She'd seen something out of the window.

"Where are they going now?"

"To the Goodleys, I expect," said Molly.

"The Goodleys? Why?"

"To complain to their parents."

"Complain to their parents?" Mum repeated in disbelief.

"They did it too," explained Max. "So they're in trouble as well. So you see, now we're just like them. Which is what you always wanted."

Max and Molly's mum went to the front window and watched Erik and Emma complain to Mr and Mrs Goodley. It wasn't exactly how she'd planned, it but just for once Max and Molly were exactly the same as the Goodleys...

She really should tell Max and Molly off of course, she told herself. And she really should dock their pocket money... But watching this...this was too good to miss.

"I will be docking your pocket money," she said, keeping her eyes firmly fixed on the scene across the road.

Max and Molly didn't say anything. This was the least they'd expected.

"Unless..." said Mum. "You promise me one thing."

"What is it?" asked Max and Molly.

"If I give you your pocket money, you must promise NOT to put it in a pension."

Max and Molly didn't need to be asked twice.

"We promise!"

Max and Molly smiled at each other. Things had turned out not too badly, after all. They may not have exactly stopped a **Viking** invasion, but they had made their mum's dream come true.

The end.

How to make Sloping Custard and Jelly Pudding

(FOR WHEN YOU'VE FINISHED PLAYING THE **SPOONS**)

You will need:

- One packet of your favourite jelly
- Some ready-made custard
- Strawberries or raspberries

Before you start, tell an adult about what you are planning to do. They may stop you from making a mess and breaking things, but as they probably paid for the ingredients, it's polite to get them involved.

1. Pour the jelly liquid into four serving glasses.

2. Place the glasses into small plastic containers on an angle so the jelly sets on a slant.

3. Put the jelly in the fridge and wait until it has set.

4. Carefully **spoon** custard on top of the jelly.

5. Add the fruit to the top!

6. Eat. **Jellicious!**

How to make sloppy custard and jelly pudding

(FOR PEOPLE WHO TELL YOU TO STOP PLAYING THE **SPOONS**)

You will need:

- One packet of jelly
- Some ready-made custard
- Strawberries or raspberries
- One pot of cream
- A handful of jelly sweets

1. Make the jelly in a big bowl

2. Put the jelly in the fridge and wait until it has set

3. Pour the other ingredients on top of the jelly

4. Use your **spoons** to mix it all together into a huge, sloppy mess!

5. Serve up **AND MAKE A RUN FOR IT!**

 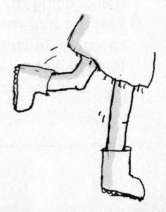

 **HANNAH SHAW** is precisely five foot five inches tall and was born some time in the 1980s. She is the brilliant author and illustrator of a number of picture books, as well an illustrator for young fiction. When she isn't drawing, writing or eating (far too many) chocolate biscuits, Hannah enjoys dog agility, dancing and making robot costumes.

DOMINIC BARKER is not sure how tall he is any more as his doctor tells him he is shrinking. He has a recurring  nightmare in which he is attacked by extremely agile dogs dressed as robots doing the conga. They hit him with chocolate biscuits. Dominic has a good idea who to blame for this...